D0097828

A TREASURY OF
PETER RABBIT
and Other Stories

BY

BEATRIX POTTER

**The Tales of Peter Rabbit, Benjamin Bunny,
Squirrel Nutkin, Two Bad Mice, and Jeremy Fisher**

Avenel Books
New York

This edition is published by Avenel Books,
distributed by Crown Publishers, Inc.

AVENEL 1979 PRINTING

f g h i j k l

THE TALE
OF
PETER RABBIT

THE TALE OF
PETER RABBIT

BY

BEATRIX POTTER

ONCE upon a time there were four little Rabbits, and their names were—
            Flopsy,
            Mopsy,
            Cotton-tail,
            and Peter.
They lived with their Mother in a sand-bank, underneath the root of a very big fir-tree.

'NOW, my dears,' said old Mrs. Rabbit one morning, 'you may go into the fields or down the lane, but don't go into Mr. McGregor's garden: your Father had an accident there; he was put in a pie by Mrs. McGregor.'

'NOW run along, and don't get into mischief. I am going out.'

THEN old Mrs. Rabbit took a basket and her umbrella, and went through the wood to the baker's. She bought a loaf of brown bread and five currant buns.

FLOPSY, Mopsy, and Cottontail, who were good little bunnies, went down the lane to gather blackberries:

BUT Peter, who was very naughty, ran straight away to Mr. McGregor's garden, and squeezed under the gate!

FIRST he ate some lettuces
and some French beans;
and then he ate some radishes;

A ND then, feeling rather
      sick, he went to look for
some parsley.

BUT round the end of a cucumber frame, whom should he meet but Mr. McGregor!

MR. McGREGOR was on his hands and knees planting out young cabbages, but he jumped up and ran after Peter, waving a rake and calling out, 'Stop thief!'

PETER was most dreadfully frightened; he rushed all over the garden, for he had forgotten the way back to the gate.

He lost one of his shoes among the cabbages, and the other shoe amongst the potatoes.

AFTER losing them, he ran on four legs and went faster, so that I think he might have got away altogether if he had not unfortunately run into a gooseberry net, and got caught by the large buttons on his jacket. It was a blue jacket with brass buttons, quite new.

PETER gave himself up for lost, and shed big tears; but his sobs were overheard by some friendly sparrows, who flew to him in great excitement, and implored him to exert himself.

MR. McGREGOR came up
with a sieve, which he
intended to pop upon the top
of Peter; but Peter wriggled
out just in time, leaving his
jacket behind him.

A ND rushed into the tool-shed, and jumped into a can. It would have been a beautiful thing to hide in, if it had not had so much water in it.

MR. McGREGOR was quite sure that Peter was somewhere in the tool-shed, perhaps hidden underneath a flower-pot. He began to turn them over carefully, looking under each.

Presently Peter sneezed — 'Kertyschoo!' Mr. McGregor was after him in no time.

AND tried to put his foot upon Peter, who jumped out of a window, upsetting three plants. The window was too small for Mr. McGregor, and he was tired of running after Peter. He went back to his work.

PETER sat down to rest; he was out of breath and trembling with fright, and he had not the least idea which way to go. Also he was very damp with sitting in that can.

After a time he began to wander about, going lippity—lippity—not very fast, and looking all round.

HE found a door in a wall; but it was locked, and there was no room for a fat little rabbit to squeeze underneath.

An old mouse was running in and out over the stone doorstep, carrying peas and beans to her family in the wood. Peter asked her the way to the gate, but she had such a large pea in her mouth that she could not answer. She only shook her head at him. Peter began to cry.

THEN he tried to find his way straight across the garden, but he became more and more puzzled. Presently, he came to a pond where Mr. McGregor filled his water-cans. A white cat was staring at some gold-fish, she sat very, very still, but now and then the tip of her tail twitched as if it were alive. Peter thought it best to go away without speaking to her; he had heard about cats from his cousin, little Benjamin Bunny.

HE went back towards the tool-shed, but suddenly, quite close to him, he heard the noise of a hoe—scr-r-ritch, scratch, scratch, scritch. Peter scuttered underneath the bushes. But presently, as nothing happened, he came out, and climbed upon a wheel-barrow and peeped over. The first thing he saw was Mr. McGregor hoeing onions. His back was turned towards Peter, and beyond him was the gate!

PETER got down very quietly off the wheel-barrow, and started running as fast as he could go, along a straight walk behind some black-currant bushes.

Mr. McGregor caught sight of him at the corner but Peter did not care. He slipped underneath the gate, and was safe at last in the wood outside the garden.

M R. McGREGOR hung up
the little jacket and the
shoes for a scare-crow to
frighten the blackbirds.

PETER never stopped running or looked behind him till he got home to the big fir-tree.

He was so tired that he flopped down upon the nice soft sand on the floor of the rabbit-hole, and shut his eyes. His mother was busy cooking; she wondered what he had done with his clothes. It was the second little jacket and pair of shoes that Peter had lost in a fortnight!

I AM sorry to say that Peter was not very well during the evening.

His mother put him to bed, and made some camomile tea; and she gave a dose of it to Peter!

'One table-spoonful to be taken at bed-time.'

BUT Flopsy, Mopsy, and Cotton-tail had bread and milk and blackberries, for supper.

THE END.

THE TALE
OF
BENJAMIN BUNNY

FOR THE CHILDREN OF SAWREY

FROM

OLD MR. BUNNY

THE TALE OF
BENJAMIN BUNNY

BY

BEATRIX POTTER

AUTHOR OF "THE TALE OF PETER RABBIT," &C.

ONE morning a little rabbit sat on a bank.

He pricked his ears and listened to the trit-trot, trit-trot of a pony.

A gig was coming along the road; it was driven by Mr. McGregor, and beside him sat Mrs. McGregor in her best bonnet.

AS soon as they had passed, little Benjamin Bunny slid down into the road, and set off—with a hop, skip, and a jump—to call upon his relations, who lived in the wood at the back of Mr. McGregor's garden.

THAT wood was full of rabbit holes; and in the neatest, sandiest hole of all lived Benjamin's aunt and his cousins—Flopsy, Mopsy, Cotton-tail, and Peter.

Old Mrs. Rabbit was a widow; she earned her living by knitting rabbit-wool mittens and muffatees (I once bought a pair at a bazaar). She also sold herbs, and rosemary tea, and rabbit-tobacco (which is what we call lavender).

LITTLE Benjamin did not very much want to see his Aunt.

He came round the back of the fir-tree, and nearly tumbled upon the top of his Cousin Peter.

PETER was sitting by him-
self. He looked poorly,
and was dressed in a red cotton
pocket-handkerchief.

"Peter," said little Benjamin, in a whisper, "who has
got your clothes?"

PETER replied, "The scarecrow in Mr. McGregor's garden," and described how he had been chased about the garden, and had dropped his shoes and coat.

Little Benjamin sat down beside his cousin and assured him that Mr. McGregor had gone out in a gig, and Mrs. McGregor also; and certainly for the day, because she was wearing her best bonnet.

PETER said he hoped that it would rain.

At this point old Mrs. Rabbit's voice was heard inside the rabbit hole, calling: "Cotton-tail! Cotton-tail! fetch some more camomile!"

Peter said he thought he might feel better if he went for a walk.

THEY went away hand in hand, and got upon the flat top of the wall at the bottom of the wood. From here they looked down into Mr. McGregor's garden. Peter's coat and shoes were plainly to be seen upon the scarecrow, topped with an old tam-o'-shanter of Mr. McGregor's.

LITTLE Benjamin said:
"It spoils people's clothes
to squeeze under a gate; the
proper way to get in is to
climb down a pear-tree."

Peter fell down head first;
but it was of no consequence,
as the bed below was newly
raked and quite soft.

IT had been sown with lettuces.

They left a great many odd little footmarks all over the bed, especially little Benjamin, who was wearing clogs.

LITTLE Benjamin said that the first thing to be done was to get back Peter's clothes, in order that they might be able to use the pocket-handkerchief.

They took them off the scarecrow. There had been rain during the night; there was water in the shoes, and the coat was somewhat shrunk.

Benjamin tried on the tam-o'-shanter, but it was too big for him.

THEN he suggested that they should fill the pocket-handkerchief with onions, as a little present for his Aunt.

Peter did not seem to be enjoying himself; he kept hearing noises.

BENJAMIN, on the contrary, was perfectly at home, and ate a lettuce leaf. He said that he was in the habit of coming to the garden with his father to get lettuces for their Sunday dinner.

(The name of little Benjamin's papa was old Mr. Benjamin Bunny.)

The lettuces certainly were very fine.

PETER did not eat anything; he said he should like to go home. Presently he dropped half the onions.

LITTLE Benjamin said that it was not possible to get back up the pear-tree with a load of vegetables. He led the way boldly towards the other end of the garden. They went along a little walk on planks, under a sunny, red brick wall.

The mice sat on their door-steps cracking cherry-stones; they winked at Peter Rabbit and little Benjamin Bunny.

PRESENTLY Peter let the pocket-handkerchief go again.

THEY got amongst flower-pots, and frames, and tubs. Peter heard noises worse than ever; his eyes were as big as lolly-pops!

He was a step or two in front of his cousin when he suddenly stopped.

THIS is what those little
rabbits saw round that
corner!

Little Benjamin took one
look, and then, in half a minute
less than no time, he hid himself and Peter and the onions
underneath a large basket. . . .

THE cat got up and stretched herself, and came and sniffed at the basket.

Perhaps she liked the smell of onions!

Anyway, she sat down upon the top of the basket.

SHE sat there for *five hours*.

*   *   *   *   *   *

I cannot draw you a picture of Peter and Benjamin underneath the basket, because it was quite dark, and because the smell of onions was fearful; it made Peter Rabbit and little Benjamin cry.

The sun got round behind the wood, and it was quite late in the afternoon; but still the cat sat upon the basket.

AT length there was a pitter-patter, pitter-patter, and some bits of mortar fell from the wall above.

The cat looked up and saw old Mr. Benjamin Bunny prancing along the top of the wall of the upper terrace.

He was smoking a pipe of rabbit-tobacco, and had a little switch in his hand.

He was looking for his son.

OLD Mr. Bunny had no opinion whatever of cats.

He took a tremendous jump off the top of the wall on to the top of the cat, and cuffed it off the basket, and kicked it into the greenhouse, scratching off a handful of fur.

The cat was too much surprised to scratch back.

WHEN old Mr. Bunny had driven the cat into the greenhouse, he locked the door.

Then he came back to the basket and took out his son Benjamin by the ears, and whipped him with the little switch.

Then he took out his nephew Peter.

THEN he took out the handkerchief of onions, and marched out of the garden.

WHEN Mr. McGregor returned about half an hour later he observed several things which perplexed him.

It looked as though some person had been walking all over the garden in a pair of clogs — only the footmarks were too ridiculously little!

Also he could not understand how the cat could have managed to shut herself up *inside* the greenhouse, locking the door upon the *outside*.

WHEN Peter got home his mother forgave him, because she was so glad to see that he had found his shoes and coat. Cotton-tail and Peter folded up the pocket-handkerchief, and old Mrs. Rabbit strung up the onions and hung them from the kitchen ceiling, with the bunches of herbs and the rabbit-tobacco.

THE END

THE TALE
OF
SQUIRREL NUTKIN

THE TALE OF

SQUIRREL NUTKIN

BY

BEATRIX POTTER

AUTHOR OF "THE TALE OF PETER RABBIT," &C.

THIS is a Tale about a tail —a tail that belonged to a little red squirrel, and his name was Nutkin.

He had a brother called Twinkleberry, and a great many cousins; they lived in a wood at the edge of a lake.

IN the middle of the lake there is an island covered with trees and nut bushes; and amongst those trees stands a hollow oak-tree, which is the house of an owl who is called Old Brown.

ONE autumn when the nuts were ripe, and the leaves on the hazel bushes were golden and green — Nutkin and Twinkleberry and all the other little squirrels came out of the wood, and down to the edge of the lake.

THEY made little rafts out of twigs, and they paddled away over the water to Owl Island to gather nuts.

Each squirrel had a little sack and a large oar, and spread out his tail for a sail.

THEY also took with them an offering of three fat mice as a present for Old Brown, and put them down upon his door-step.

Then Twinkleberry and the other little squirrels each made a low bow, and said politely—

"Old Mr. Brown, will you favor us with permission to gather nuts upon your island?"

BUT Nutkin was excessive-ly impertinent in his manners. He bobbed up and down like a little red *cherry,* singing—

"Riddle me, riddle me, rot-tot-tote!
A little wee man in a red, red coat!
A staff in his hand, and a stone in his throat;
If you'll tell me this riddle, I'll give you a
    groat."

Now this riddle is as old as the hills; Mr. Brown paid no attention whatever to Nutkin.

He shut his eyes obstinately and went to sleep.

THE squirrels filled their little sacks with nuts, and sailed away home in the evening.

BUT next morning they all came back again to Owl Island; and Twinkleberry and the others brought a fine fat mole, and laid it on the stone in front of Old Brown's doorway, and said—

"Mr. Brown, will you favor us with your gracious permission to gather some more nuts?"

BUT Nutkin, who had no respect, began to dance up and down, tickling old Mr. Brown with a *nettle* and singing—

> "Old Mr. B! Riddle-me-ree!
> Hitty Pitty within the wall,
> Hitty Pitty without the wall;
> If you touch Hitty Pitty,
> Hitty Pitty will bite you!"

Mr. Brown woke up suddenly and carried the mole into his house.

HE shut the door in Nut-
kin's face. Presently a
little thread of blue *smoke*
from a wood fire came up
from the top of the tree, and
Nutkin peeped through the
key-hole and sang—

"A house full, a hole full!
And you cannot gather a bowl-full!"

THE squirrels searched for nuts all over the island and filled their little sacks.

But Nutkin gathered oak-apples — yellow and scarlet — and sat upon a beech-stump playing marbles, and watching the door of Old Mr. Brown.

ON the third day the squirrels got up very early and went fishing; they caught seven fat minnows as a present for Old Brown.

They paddled over the lake and landed under a crooked chestnut-tree on Owl Island.

TWINKLEBERRY and six other little squirrels each carried a fat minnow; but Nutkin, who had no nice manners, brought no present at all. He ran in front, singing—

"The man in the wilderness said to me,
'How many strawberries grow in the sea?'
I answered him as I thought good—
'As many red herrings as grow in the wood.'"

But Old Mr. Brown took no interest in riddles — not even when the answer was provided for him.

ON the fourth day the squirrels brought a present of six fat beetles, which were as good as plums in *plum-pudding* for Old Brown. Each beetle was wrapped up carefully in a dockleaf, fastened with a pine-needle pin.

But Nutkin sang as rudely as ever—

"Old Mr. B! riddle-me-ree!
Flour of England, fruit of Spain,
Met together in a shower of rain;
Put in a bag tied round with a string,
If you'll tell me this riddle I'll give you a
        ring!"

Which was ridiculous of Nutkin, because he had not got any ring to give to Old Brown.

THE other squirrels hunted up and down the nut bushes; but Nutkin gathered robin's pin-cushions off a briar bush, and stuck them full of pine-needle pins.

ON the fifth day the squirrels brought a present of wild honey; it was so sweet and sticky that they licked their fingers as they put it down upon the stone. They had stolen it out of a bumble *bees*' nest on the tippitty top of the hill.

But Nutkin skipped up and down, singing—

"Hum-a-bum!   buzz!   buzz!   Hum-a-bum
            buzz!
    As I went over Tipple-tine
    I met a flock of bonny swine;
Some yellow-nacked, some yellow backed!
    They were the very bonniest swine
    That e'er went over Tipple-tine."

OLD Mr. Brown turned up his eyes in disgust at the impertinence of Nutkin.

But he ate up the honey!

THE squirrels filled their little sacks with nuts.

But Nutkin sat upon a big flat rock, and played ninepins with a crab apple and green fir-cones.

ON the sixth day, which was Saturday, the squirrels came again for the last time; they brought a new laid *egg* in a little rush basket as a last parting present for Old Brown.

But Nutkin ran in front laughing, and shouting—

"Humpty Dumpty lies in the beck,
  With a white counterpane round his neck,
  Forty doctors and forty wrights,
  Cannot put Humpty Dumpty to rights!"

NOW Old Mr. Brown took an interest in eggs; he opened one eye and shut it again. But still he did not speak.

NUTKIN became more and more impertin- ent—

Old Mr. B! Old Mr. B!
Hickamore, Hackamore, on the King's
        kitchen door;
All the King's horses, and all the
        King's men,
Couldn't drive Hickamore, Hackamore,
Off the King's kitchen door."

Nutkin danced up and down like a *sunbeam*, but still Old Brown said nothing at all.

NUTKIN began again—
"Arthur O'Bower has broken his band,
He comes roaring up the land!
The King of Scots with all his power,
Cannot turn Arthur of the Bower!"

Nutkin made a whirring noise to sound like the *wind*, and he took a running jump right onto the head of Old Brown! . . . .

Then all at once there was a flutterment and a scufflllement and a loud "Squeak!"

The other squirrels scuttered away into the bushes.

WHEN they came back very cautiously peeping round the tree—there was Old Brown sitting on his door-step, quite still, with his eyes closed, as if nothing had happened.

* * * * * *

But Nutkin was in his waistcoat pocket!

THIS looks like the end of
the story; but it isn't.

OLD BROWN carried Nutkin into his house, and held him up by the tail, intending to skin him; but Nutkin pulled so very hard that his tail broke in two, and he dashed up the staircase and escaped out of the attic window.

AND to this day if you meet Nutkin up a tree and ask him a riddle, he will throw sticks at you and stamp his feet and scold, and shout—

"C u c k - cuck-cuck-cur-r-r cuck-k-k!"

THE END.

THE TALE
OF
TWO BAD MICE

THE TALE OF
TWO BAD MICE

BY

BEATRIX POTTER

AUTHOR OF "THE TALE OF PETER RABBIT," &C.

ONCE upon a time there was a very beautiful doll's house; it was red brick with white windows, and it had real muslin curtains and a front door and a chimney.

IT belonged to two Dolls called Lucinda and Jane; at least it belonged to Lucinda, but she never ordered meals.

Jane was the Cook; but she never did any cooking, because the dinner had been bought ready-made, in a box full of shavings.

THERE were two red lob-
sters, and a ham, a fish,
a pudding, and some pears and
oranges.

They would not come off the
plates, but they were extremely
beautiful.

ONE morning Lucinda and Jane had gone out for a drive in the doll's perambulator. There was no one in the nursery, and it was very quiet. Presently there was a little scuffling, scratching noise in a corner near the fireplace, where there was a hole under the skirting-board.

Tom Thumb put out his head for a moment, and then popped it in again.

Tom Thumb was a mouse.

A MINUTE afterwards Hunca Munca, his wife, put her head out, too; and when she saw that there was no one in the nursery, she ventured out on the oilcloth under the coal-box.

THE doll's house stood at the other side of the fireplace. Tom Thumb and Hunca Munca went cautiously across the hearth-rug. They pushed the front door—it was not fast.

TOM THUMB and Hunca Munca went up-stairs and peeped into the dining-room. Then they squeaked with joy!

Such a lovely dinner was laid out upon the table! There were tin spoons, and lead knives and forks, and two dolly-chairs —all *so* convenient!

TOM THUMB set to work at once to carve the ham. It was a beautiful shiny yellow, streaked with red.

The knife crumpled up and hurt him; he put his finger in his mouth.

"It is not boiled enough; it is hard. You have a try, Hunca Munca."

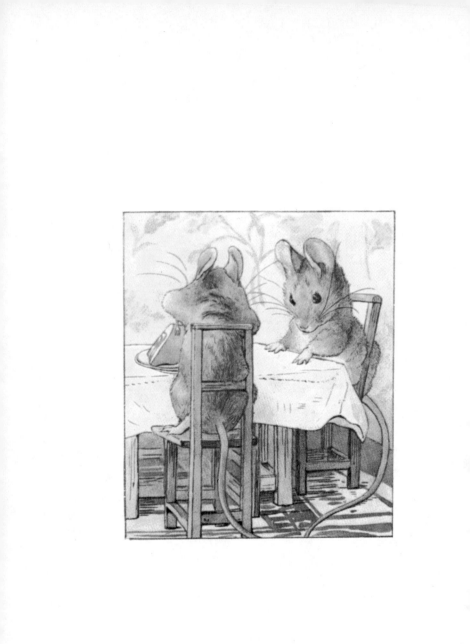

HUNCA MUNCA stood up in her chair, and chopped at the ham with another lead knife.

"It's as hard as the hams at the cheesemonger's," said Hunca Munca.

THE ham broke off the plate with a jerk, and rolled under the table.

"Let it alone," said Tom Thumb; "give me some fish, Hunca Munca!"

HUNCA MUNCA tried every tin spoon in turn; the fish was glued to the dish.

Then Tom Thumb lost his temper. He put the ham in the middle of the floor, and hit it with the tongs and with the shovel—bang, bang, smash, smash!

The ham flew all into pieces, for underneath the shiny paint it was made of nothing but plaster!

THEN there was no end to the rage and disappointment of Tom Thumb and Hunca Munca. They broke up the pudding, the lobsters, the pears, and the oranges.

As the fish would not come off the plate, they put it into the red-hot crinkly paper fire in the kitchen; but it would not burn either.

TOM THUMB went up the kitchen chimney and looked out at the top—there was no soot

WHILE Tom Thumb was up the chimney, Hunca Munca had another disappointment. She found some tiny canisters upon the dresser, labeled "Rice," "Coffee," "Sago"; but when she turned them upside down there was nothing inside except red and blue beads.

THEN those mice set to work to do all the mischief they could—especially Tom Thumb! He took Jane's clothes out of the chest of drawers in her bedroom, and he threw them out of the top-floor window.

But Hunca Munca had a frugal mind. After pulling half the feathers out of Lucinda's bolster, she remembered that she herself was in want of a feather-bed.

WITH Tom Thumb's assistance she carried the bolster down-stairs and across the hearth-rug. It was difficult to squeeze the bolster into the mouse-hole; but they managed it somehow.

THEN Hunca Munca went back and fetched a chair, a bookcase, a bird-cage, and several small odds and ends. The bookcase and the bird-cage refused to go into the mouse-hole.

HUNCA MUNCA left them behind the coal-box, and went to fetch a cradle.

HUNCA MUNCA was just returning with another chair, when suddenly there was a noise of talking outside upon the landing. The mice rushed back to their hole, and the dolls came into the nursery.

WHAT a sight met the eyes of Jane and Lucinda!

Lucinda sat upon the upset kitchen stove and stared, and Jane leaned against the kitchen dresser and smiled; but neither of them made any remark.

THE bookcase and the bird-cage were rescued from under the coal-box; but Hunca Munca has got the cradle and some of Lucinda's clothes.

SHE also has some useful pots and pans, and several other things.

THE little girl that the doll's house belonged to said: "I will get a doll dressed like a policeman!"

BUT the nurse said: "I will set a mouse-trap!"

SO that is the story of the two Bad Mice. But they were not so very, very naughty after all, because Tom Thumb paid for everything he broke.

He found a crooked sixpence under the hearth-rug; and upon Christmas Eve he and Hunca Munca stuffed it into one of the stockings of Lucinda and Jane.

A ND very early every morning—before anybody is
awake—Hunca Munca comes
with her dust-pan and her
broom to sweep the Dollies'
house!

THE END

THE TALE
OF
MR. JEREMY FISHER

THE TALE OF
MR. JEREMY FISHER

BY

BEATRIX POTTER

Author of "The Tale of Peter Rabbit," Etc.

FOR
STEPHANIE
FROM
COUSIN B.

ONCE upon a time there was a frog called Mr. Jeremy Fisher; he lived in a little damp house amongst the buttercups at the edge of a pond.

THE water was all slippy-sloppy in the larder and in the back passage.

But Mr. Jeremy liked getting his feet wet; nobody ever scolded him, and he never caught a cold!

HE was quite pleased when he looked out and saw large drops of rain, splashing in the pond—

"I WILL get some worms and go fishing and catch a dish of minnows for my dinner," said Mr. Jeremy Fisher. "If I catch more than five fish, I will invite my friends Mr. Alderman Ptolemy Tortoise and Sir Isaac Newton. The Alderman, however, eats salad."

MR. JEREMY put on a macintosh, and a pair of shiny galoshes; he took his rod and basket, and set off with enormous hops to the place where he kept his boat.

THE boat was round and green, and very like the other lily-leaves. It was tied to a water-plant in the middle of the pond.

MR. JEREMY took a reed pole, and pushed the boat out into open water. "I know a good place for minnows," said Mr. Jeremy Fisher.

MR. JEREMY stuck his pole into the mud and fastened the boat to it.

Then he settled himself cross-legged and arranged his fishing tackle. He had the dearest little red float. His rod was a tough stalk of grass, his line was a fine long white horse-hair, and he tied a little wriggling worm at the end.

THE rain trickled down his back, and for nearly an hour he stared at the float.

"This is getting tiresome, I think I should like some lunch," said Mr. Jeremy Fisher.

HE punted back again amongst the water-plants, and took some lunch out of his basket.

"I will eat a butterfly sandwich, and wait till the shower is over," said Mr. Jeremy Fisher.

A GREAT big water-beetle came up underneath the lily leaf and tweaked the toe of one of his galoshes.

Mr. Jeremy crossed his legs up shorter, out of reach, and went on eating his sandwich.

ONCE or twice something moved about with a rustle and a splash amongst the rushes at the side of the pond.

"I trust that is not a rat," said Mr. Jeremy Fisher; "I think I had better get away from here."

MR. JEREMY shoved the boat out again a little way, and dropped in the bait. There was a bite almost directly; the float gave a tremendous bobbit!

"A minnow! a minnow! I have him by the nose!" cried Mr. Jeremy Fisher, jerking up his rod.

BUT what a horrible surprise! Instead of a smooth fat minnow, Mr. Jeremy landed little Jack Sharp the stickleback, covered with spines!

THE stickleback floundered about the boat, pricking and snapping until he was quite out of breath. Then he jumped back into the water.

AND a shoal of other little fishes put their heads out, and laughed at Mr. Jeremy Fisher.

AND while Mr. Jeremy sat disconsolately on the edge of his boat—sucking his sore fingers and peering down into the water—a *much* worse thing happened; a really *frightful* thing it would have been, if Mr. Jeremy had not been wearing a macintosh!

A GREAT big enormous trout came up — ker-pflop-p-p-p! with a splash— and it seized Mr. Jeremy with a snap, "Ow! Ow! Ow!" — and then it turned and dived down to the bottom of the pond!

BUT the trout was so displeased with the taste of the macintosh, that in less than half a minute it spat him out again; and the only thing it swallowed was Mr. Jeremy's galoshes.

MR. JEREMY bounced up
to the surface of the
water, like a cork and the
bubbles out of a soda water
bottle; and he swam with
all his might to the edge of
the pond.

HE scrambled out on the first bank he came to, and he hopped home across the meadow with his macintosh all in tatters.

"WHAT a mercy that was not a pike!" said Mr. Jeremy Fisher. "I have lost my rod and basket; but it does not much matter, for I am sure I should never have dared to go fishing again!"

HE put some sticking plaster on his fingers, and his friends both came to dinner. He could not offer them fish, but he had something else in his larder.

SIR ISAAC NEWTON wore his black and gold waistcoat.

AND Mr. Alderman Ptolemy Tortoise brought a salad with him in a string bag.

AND instead of a nice dish of minnows—they had a roasted grasshopper with lady-bird sauce; which frogs consider a beautiful treat; but *I* think it must have been nasty!

THE END